~The New Adventures of~
MARY-KATE & ASHLEY

The Case Of The
CLUE AT THE ZOO

Look for more great books in

~The New Adventures of~
MARY-KATE & ASHLEY™

series:

The Case Of The Great Elephant Escape
The Case Of The Summer Camp Caper
The Case Of The Surfing Secret
The Case Of The Green Ghost
The Case Of The Big Scare Mountain Mystery
The Case Of The Slam Dunk Mystery
The Case Of The Rock Star's Secret
The Case Of The Cheerleading Camp Mystery
The Case Of The Flying Phantom
The Case Of The Creepy Castle
The Case Of The Golden Slipper
The Case Of The Flapper 'Napper
The Case Of The High Seas Secret
The Case Of The Logical I Ranch
The Case Of The Dog Camp Mystery
The Case Of The Screaming Scarecrow
The Case Of The Jingle Bell Jinx
The Case Of The Game Show Mystery
The Case Of The Mall Mystery
The Case Of The Weird Science Mystery
The Case Of Camp Crooked Lake
The Case Of The Giggling Ghost
The Case Of The Candy Cane Clue
The Case Of The Hollywood Who-Done-It
The Case Of The Sundae Surprise
The Case Of Clue's Circus Caper
The Case Of Camp Pom-Pom
The Case Of The Tattooed Cat
The Case Of The Nutcracker Ballet

and coming soon

The Case Of The Easter Egg Race

The Case Of The
CLUE AT THE ZOO

by Judy Katschke

📖HarperEntertainment
An Imprint of HarperCollins*Publishers*

A PARACHUTE PRESS BOOK

PARACHUTE PRESS

Parachute Publishing, L.L.C.
156 Fifth Avenue
New York, NY 10010

DUALSTAR PUBLICATIONS

Dualstar Publications
c/o Thorne and Company
A Professional Law Corporation
1801 Century Park East
Los Angeles, CA 90067

HarperEntertainment

An Imprint of HarperCollins*Publishers*
10 East 53rd Street, New York, NY 10022

First printing: January 2004

Printed in the United States of America

10 9 8 7 6 5 4 3 2 1

1

ZOO GONE WILD!

"I can't believe a real-live panda is coming to live at our zoo!" our friend Tim Park said. "Is that cool or what?" He pointed toward the zoo gate. A huge poster of Mei Ling, the famous Chinese panda, hung next to it.

"Way cool," I agreed. "But Mei Ling isn't here yet, Tim."

"The directors of the Chinese zoo have to approve our zoo first," my twin sister, Ashley, reminded him. "That's why Mr. and

Mrs. Tang and their son, Shen, came all the way from China. To take a tour of our zoo."

"They'll like it here for sure," our friend Samantha Samuels said. "Our zoo has the best animals in the world!"

Tim, Samantha, Ashley, and I are on the Zoo Crew. It's a club for kids who want to learn about animals. Every Saturday we come to the zoo and learn how to take care of them.

Like last week Ashley whipped up a berry-and-seed mix for the parrots. I spread fresh hay in the petting zoo. Samantha tied ropes in knots for the apes and monkeys to play with. And Tim cleaned out the bird-cages. He had to hold his nose the whole time!

But today is going to be totally different. That's because today is Mei Ling Day! At eight o'clock, Mr. Farley, the zoo director, gave a big breakfast in honor of the Tangs. The Zoo Crew wasn't invited to that, but it's okay. Because at nine o'clock we are all invited to join the tour!

Samantha tugged the sleeve of my Zoo Crew T-shirt.

"Mary-Kate," she said, "look who else showed up for Mei Ling Day—Toby Tolliver!"

I turned to look where Samantha was pointing. A boy with spiky brown hair was standing right inside the zoo gate. He held up a sign that read THIS ZOO STINKS!

"Give me a break." I groaned.

Toby used to be on the Zoo Crew too. But he spent more time playing pranks than taking care of the animals. So last week our leader, Wally, kicked him off the Zoo Crew.

"Remember when Toby went swimming in the seal pond?" Tim said.

"And taught the parrots to call Wally a doodlehead?" Samantha added.

"I just remember how mad Toby was

when he left," Ashley said. "Let's go see what he's doing here."

We walked through the gate. Toby wasn't wearing his Zoo Crew T-shirt like the rest of us. Instead, he wore a black T-shirt and jeans and had a purple backpack slung over his shoulder.

"What are you doing here, Toby?" I asked.

"Can't you read?" Toby said. He jabbed his sign. "I'm letting the Tangs know the truth about this dumb zoo!"

"But Wally told you to leave the zoo and never come back," Tim said.

"He meant the Zoo *Crew*, smarty," Toby said. "Anyone can come to the zoo—including me!"

Toby turned to the guests coming through the gate. "This zoo stinks!" he shouted.

"Ignore him," Ashley muttered.

The four of us walked farther into the

zoo. The paths are named after animals, like Sloth Street, Rhinoceros Road, and my favorite—Warthog Way!

"Wow!" I said as we passed under a balloon arch. There were posters of Mei Ling everywhere. All the gift carts were selling stuffed pandas and Mei Ling T-shirts. There was even a guy walking around in a panda suit!

"Come on," Ashley said. "The tour is starting on Aardvark Avenue"—she glanced at her watch—"in exactly five minutes!"

When we reached Aardvark Avenue, we saw a crowd of people standing around a platform. Some were waving stuffed pandas on sticks. Others had on panda masks. I could see Wally and some other zookeepers in the crowd. That meant the breakfast was probably over.

"It's a panda party!" Tim exclaimed.

"And those must be the Tangs!" Ashley said, pointing.

A man, a woman, and a boy were standing on the platform next to Mr. Farley, the zoo director. Mr. Tang wore a beige suit. Mrs. Tang had on a white dress and a straw hat. Their son, Shen, wore shorts and a polo shirt.

Mr. Farley faced the crowd and spoke into a microphone. "If Mei Ling were here, she'd probably say 'This is the zoo for me,'" he announced. "So what are we waiting for? Let the tour begin!"

A band started playing "If I Could Talk to the Animals." Chinese dancers waved colorful ribbons in the air. Mr. Farley led the Tangs and the guests away from Aardvark Avenue and straight up Hippopotamus Lane.

I waved to some of the other Zoo Crew kids in the crowd: Robbie Tarnoff, Melissa Han, and Felicia Montrose.

"As you will see," Mr. Farley continued, "each animal lives in an area that matches its own natural habitat. In fact, our zoo—"

"Stinks!" a voice yelled. "This zoo stinks!"

I groaned under my breath. Terrible Toby was marching behind us with his big nasty sign!

"Kids and their jokes." Mr. Farley chuckled nervously. "Why don't we start the tour with the Reptile House? We have a very interesting variety of snakes!"

The Tangs walked up ahead with Mr. Farley. Shen lagged behind. He was hanging his head and dragging his feet.

"Let's go over and say hi," I told the others.

Shen looked surprised when we caught up with him.

"Hi! I'm Mary-Kate Olsen, and this is my sister Ashley," I said. "And these are our friends Tim and Samantha."

"You're really going to like our zoo, Shen," Ashley said. "So will Mei Ling."

"But I don't want Mei Ling to come

here," Shen said. "I visit her every day at our zoo at home. She's like a pet to me!"

No wonder Shen looked sad. Ashley and I would be sad too if someone were giving away our dog, Clue!

"You'll like the animals here," Tim said, trying to change the subject from Mei Ling. "We have a real Bengal tiger, lions, a rhinoceros—"

Shen's eyes widened. "Snakes!"

"We have those too," I said.

"No!" Shen pointed over my shoulder and shouted, "Snakes on the loose! Snakes on the loose!"

I spun around and gasped. There were snakes slithering out of the Reptile House! Lots and lots of them!

WHO LET THE SNAKES OUT?

"**S**nakes?" Mrs. Tang gasped. "Where?"

Mr. and Mrs. Tang glanced down and shrieked. Little green snakes were wiggling right over their shoes!

Ashley and I had learned all about reptiles in the Zoo Crew, so we knew they were harmless garter snakes. But what were they doing outside their tanks?

"Th-this has never happened before!" Mr. Farley stammered. "Our snakes are kept in tanks with very heavy lids. And they're watched closely by our snake handler, Jasmine!"

"Don't worry, Mr. Farley!" Jasmine called as she ran toward the snakes. "I'll put them back!"

"Well!" Mr. Tang said. "This has never happened at *our* zoo!"

"I told you this zoo is bad news!" Toby laughed meanly. "You'd better keep Mei Ling in China!"

Tim glared at Toby. "Put a sock in it, Toby!"

Mr. Farley cleared his throat. "Let's continue the tour, shall we?" he suggested. "You'll see that the rest of our zoo is run like a tight ship."

Mr. and Mrs. Tang followed Mr. Farley up the path. They were muttering something in Chinese that I didn't understand. But Shen was giggling to himself.

At least Shen is in a better mood, I thought.

We walked away from the Reptile House and up Hippopotamus Lane. It was the same path we took to the Zoo Crew Hut every morning.

"Now," Mr. Farley announced cheerily, "we're coming up to our petting zoo. We have lambs, llamas, burros, and—"

BAAAAAA! BAAAAAA!

"Sheep!" Shen shouted.

My mouth dropped open as a sheep charged up the path—straight toward Mr. Tang!

"Oof!" Mr. Tang grunted as the sheep butted his stomach. He flew back and landed on the ground with a thud!

"Mr. Farley!" a zookeeper shouted as he ran toward us. "Someone left the petting zoo gate wide open!"

Ashley, Tim, Samantha, and I jumped aside as sheep, llamas, and burros charged up the path. Two zookeepers ran after them, trying to round them all up!

"Mr. Farley!" Mrs. Tang cried. "Are your animals allowed to run free?"

"I—I—I—" Mr. Farley stammered. "I don't get it!"

Mr. Farley helped Mr. Tang stand up. "Please, sir!" he said. "The zoo isn't like this every day. As I said, it's run like a tight ship!"

"Yeah—a *sinking* ship!" Toby laughed.

Ashley and I shot Toby a sharp look. It was bad enough he had to show up, but did he have to be so creepy?

"Let's move on to the Orangutan Den," Mr. Farley told the Tangs. "So you can see what our zoo is *really* like!"

We reached the Orangutan Den and looked through the wire fence. Oh, no! The orangutans were spraying one another with water blasters and tossing Frisbees back and forth across the den!

"They're not playing with the rope toys I made for them," Samantha complained. "They've got toys from the gift shop!"

Samantha was right. The water blasters were shaped like elephants. The Frisbees made animal noises. Everyone on the Zoo Crew had gotten those toys when we joined. But how did they get into the Orangutan Den?

"Mr. Farley!" Mrs. Tang looked shocked. "Your monkeys play with Frisbees? And water squirters?"

All of a sudden a voice cried out—

"Hate Mei Ling! Hate Mei Ling! Hate Mei Ling!"

Everyone whirled around. A parrot in a nearby cage was chanting "Hate Mei Ling" over and over. Next to the cage was a whole wall of posters of Mei Ling. But the posters all had big brown X's drawn across Mei Ling's face!

"That does it!" Mr. Tang said. "This zoo is no place for our Mei Ling!"

"We are going back to China," Mrs. Tang announced.

"Ye-es!" Shen cheered.

Wally squeezed his way through the crowd. He was wearing his usual Zoo Crew leader uniform—a Zoo Crew T-shirt, green khaki pants, and a matching green cap.

"Mr. and Mrs. Tang, our zoo isn't always like this," Wally said. "The zookeepers and I checked the whole place before the breakfast this morning and everything was fine. Someone must be playing a prank or—"

"I'm afraid it's too late," Mr. Tang said firmly. "This isn't a zoo. It's a *circus*!"

"Come, Shen," Mrs. Tang said. She grabbed his hand. Then the whole Tang family marched back up the path.

"Come baaaaack!" Mr. Farley called as he raced after them. "We'll get to the bottom of this and fix everything!"

"Ha ha!" Toby laughed as he walked away. "There won't be any panda in this zoo. That's for sure!"

Nobody else thought it was funny.

Getting Mei Ling to come to our zoo was everyone's dream. Now it was one big nightmare!

"Bummer," Tim said, shaking his head.

"How did all this happen?" Samantha wondered.

"Somebody must have done this on purpose," I said.

"I think so too," Ashley agreed. "The toys didn't get into the Orangutan Den by themselves. And the *X*'s couldn't have gotten on Mei Ling's posters like magic."

Melissa, Robbie, and Felicia walked over.

"We came *so* close to getting Mei Ling!" Melissa said.

"Now we'll never have our own panda." Robbie sighed.

"At least we still have Chucky the Chummy Chimp!" Felicia said. "He's a *star*!"

Chucky is famous. He is a chimpanzee who knows sign language. And Felicia is Chucky's biggest fan.

"Okay, Zoo Crew," Wally called out. "I'll need your help tearing down all those messed-up posters."

Ashley and I were about to join the others, but Wally turned to us and said, "I have a different job for you two. I want you to find out who wrecked our zoo—and why."

"In other words," I said with a smile, "you want us to solve another mystery!"

"You got it!" Wally said, smiling back.

Ashley and I are detectives. We run the Olsen and Olsen Detective Agency. We have been solving mysteries ever since our great-grandma Olive gave us a bunch of detective books to read. She is a world-famous detective.

"It would be great if you solved the case before the Tangs go back to China," Wally added, "so we can prove to them that our zoo isn't always like this."

Tim and Samantha began jumping up and down.

"Another case for the Trenchcoat Twins!" Samantha declared.

"Woo hoo!" Tim cheered.

Our friends always love it when we solve mysteries. Probably because they love to help!

"So, will you take on the case?" Wally asked us.

"Yes!" Ashley said quickly. "We want Mei Ling to come to this zoo too. And we want to find that creepy zoo-wrecker—whoever it is!"

"That shouldn't take too long," I said.

Ashley stared at me. "Why not?" she asked.

"Because," I said slowly, "I'm pretty sure I know who the zoo-wrecker is!"

CLUE? PE-EW!

"**W**ho did it, Mary-Kate?" Tim asked.

I pointed to Toby Tolliver. He was standing by the zoo gate waving his sign. "I think it was Toby!" I said. "He was mad at Wally for kicking him off the Zoo Crew. He might have trashed the zoo to get even."

I expected Ashley to agree right away. But she shook her head instead. "We don't have any proof it was Toby," Ashley said.

"Here we go again!" I sighed.

Ashley and I both have strawberry-blond

hair and blue eyes. We're about the same height. But when it comes to solving mysteries, we're as different as seals and giraffes! Ashley likes to solve each case one step at a time. And I'm usually three steps ahead of myself!

"Can you start on the case right away?" Wally asked.

"Are you kidding?" Tim asked. "We're on it!"

"We're supposed to help tear down the posters, Tim," Samantha said. "Remember?"

"Oh, yeah." Tim sighed.

Tim and Samantha left with Wally. But I knew they would find a way to help us with the case sooner or later.

"Okay," Ashley said, "let's get to work!"

We sat down on a bench carved with animal heads. I wiggled out of my special red detective backpack and placed it on my lap. Ashley pulled out her detective notebook. I grabbed my mini–tape recorder and checked the batteries. Maybe it would come in handy later.

"What do we know so far?" I asked.

"Wally checked out the zoo before the Tangs' breakfast and everything was fine," Ashley said. "So the crimes must have happened while everyone was at the breakfast."

"Maybe the zoo-wrecker is someone who works at the zoo," I said.

"But everyone who works at the zoo was at the Tangs' breakfast," Ashley said.

"Unless the zoo-wrecker sneaked out of the breakfast to trash the zoo!" I said.

Ashley began drawing in her detective pad. It looked like a connect-the-dot game!

"What are you doing?" I asked.

"I'm drawing a diagram of all the places that were wrecked," Ashley explained. "The Reptile House, the petting zoo, the Orangutan Den, and the fence with the crossed-out posters of Mei Ling."

"Hmm," I said, studying the diagram.

"They're all on Hippopotamus Lane. The same path our Zoo Crew Hut is on."

Ashley looked at me. "Maybe you were right, Mary-Kate," she said. "Maybe the zoo-wrecker *is* a Zoo Crew kid. . . ."

"A Zoo Crew kid like *Toby*," I said. "He could have used his pass to get into the zoo early. And he has all the toys the orangutans were playing with too. He could have thrown them over the fence to the orangutans!"

"True," Ashley said. "But we still need—"

"Proof," I filled in. "I know, I know."

Ashley wrote Toby's name down in her detective notebook. "Let's go look for clues," she suggested. "We need to go to all the places that were wrecked."

"Eee, eee, eee!" a voice screeched.

We looked up. Chucky the Chummy Chimp came running toward us. He wore a red baseball cap that was turned around so that the brim faced the back.

A woman dressed in khaki shorts and a

white shirt ran after Chucky. It was Jean Goodrich, the woman who taught Chucky sign language. Jean is a primatologist. She studies primates, which are animals such as gorillas, orangutans, and chimpanzees like Chucky. The kids on the Zoo Crew call her the Monkey Lady—but Jean doesn't mind. She likes it when we call her that.

"Chucky, not so fast!" Jean called.

Ashley and I stood up. Chucky jumped up and down in front of the bench and started waving his fingers over his head.

"Is Chucky signing something?" Ashley asked excitedly.

"Chucky is signing the word *snake*," Jean said. "But I have no idea why."

"Eee, eee, eee!" Chucky cried.

Jean gently took Chucky's hand. "Come along, Chucky. It's time to visit Shen Tang. He can't wait to meet you."

She and Chucky walked away. Chucky turned and waved to us. We waved back.

"*Snake* must be Chucky's new word," I said. "He loves sharing new words with us."

"He also gave me an idea," Ashley said. "Let's search the Reptile House first. Maybe we can find some clues there."

I packed my mini-recorder into the back-pack. Then we headed up Hippopotamus Lane. People were looking at the animals and buying balloons as they did every Saturday.

As we neared the Reptile House I saw two signs on the door. One read NO TAPPING ON GLASS TANKS. NO FOOD ALLOWED. That sign was always there. But today there was a new sign hanging on the door. It read SORRY! CLOSED TO GUESTS!

"Jasmine probably wants to make sure all the snakes are in their tanks," I said.

"A very good idea!" Ashley said.

We didn't mind little green garter snakes, but we definitely didn't want to meet one of the big poisonous ones outside its tank!

I knocked on the door. There was no answer.

"How can we go inside if it's closed?" Ashley asked.

"It's closed to *guests*," I pointed out. "And we're not guests—we're the Zoo Crew!"

The door wasn't locked, so we opened it and walked right in. It was dark in there as usual, so we left the door wide open. Then Ashley and I looked around for clues.

All the garter snakes were back in their tanks. We couldn't find anything suspicious. Then I saw something strange. . . .

"Check it out, Ashley!" I pointed down to the cement floor. "Those ants are all marching in the same direction."

We squatted down and studied the ants. "It's like a little ant parade," Ashley said. "I wonder where they're going."

Ashley and I followed the ants. They were marching between two snake tanks. I peeked inside the narrow space. On the floor was a smelly banana peel covered with hungry ants!

"Yuck!" I said. "How gross is that?"

"Some messy guest probably dropped it," Ashley said, shaking her head.

"But the Reptile House was closed to guests all morning," I said.

Ashley raised an eyebrow. "Maybe the *zoo-wrecker* was eating a banana before he let the snakes out," she said. She was about to reach into my backpack for the detective notebook when—

SLAM!

We both jumped. The Reptile House was totally dark!

Ashley and I felt our way to the door. But when I tried to push it open—

"It's locked!" I exclaimed. "We're locked in!"

4

TRAPPED!

Ashley and I both tried pushing the door. But it was no use. The heavy wooden door wouldn't budge!

"Who would want to lock us in here?" I asked in the dark.

"Maybe the zoo-wrecker locked us in," Ashley said, "so we'd be out of the way!"

It was too dark to see the snakes. But I knew they were there: rattlesnakes . . . cobras . . . a big black mamba!

"Ashley?" I gulped. "What if some of the

snakes are still . . . you know . . . loose?"

"Snakes . . . loose?" Ashley squeaked.

I felt goose bumps all over—especially on my legs. Maybe there were snakes slithering up my legs right now. . . .

"Hey!" I shouted as I pounded on the door. "Get us out of heeeeeere!"

"Somebody!" Ashley yelled. "Helllp!"

No one heard us. Ashley and I stepped way back. Then we charged toward the door. But just as we were about to slam against it, the door flew wide open.

"Whoaaa!" Ashley and I cried as we fell forward. We landed on our hands and knees. Lucky for us it was on the grass.

"Are you girls okay?" a voice asked.

I blinked my eyes as they adjusted to the light. Wally was standing over us.

"We're fine, thanks," I said.

"How did you find us, Wally?" Ashley asked.

"I was passing by and heard you two

screaming," Wally replied. "How did you get locked in the Reptile House?"

I adjusted my backpack as we stood up.

"We were searching for clues," I explained, "and someone locked the door."

"We haven't found the zoo-wrecker yet," Ashley said, "but we did find a great clue."

Ashley ran inside to get the banana peel. She looked grossed out as she carried it out between two fingers.

"A banana peel?" Wally asked. He scratched his head under his zookeeper hat. "What kind of clue is that?"

"We think the zoo-wrecker dropped it before he freed the snakes," I said. "Did you see anyone eating a banana in the zoo this morning, Wally?"

"Come to think of it," Wally said slowly, "Shen Tang was eating a banana when he skipped out of the breakfast."

"You mean Shen left the breakfast *early*?" I asked.

"With a *banana*?" Ashley asked.

Wally nodded. "He was also carrying a bag filled with zoo toys," he said. "Mr. Farley gave it to him as a welcome present."

Ashley and I stared at each other.

"Zoo toys?" I gasped. "Those were the toys the orangutans were playing with!"

"Why did Shen leave, Wally?" Ashley asked.

"I don't know," Wally said. "He left before I could even say hi."

A family came over to ask directions. While Wally helped them, I turned to Ashley.

"I don't get it, Mary-Kate," Ashley said. "Why would Shen Tang want to trash our zoo?"

I didn't get it either. Shen was such a nice kid. But then I remembered what he had told us earlier on the tour.

"Shen doesn't want Mei Ling to leave China," I said, "so maybe he wrecked our zoo so that his parents wouldn't like it here!"

"Let's go talk to Shen," Ashley said. "He's probably at Mr. Farley's house. That's where the Tangs are staying."

I pulled a plastic bag from my backpack and dropped the stinky banana peel into it. We always keep our clues in plastic bags. That's something we learned from our great-grandma Olive.

We found Mr. Farley's house near the zoo gate. It looked like a normal white house with green shutters. But the bushes around it were trimmed to look like zoo animals. There was a lion, a bear, a gorilla, and lots of different kinds of birds.

"There's Shen," Ashley said in a low voice.

Shen was standing outside the house with Jean and Chucky. Chucky was signing something to Shen—and Shen was signing back!

"Hi, Shen," I called as we walked over. "Do you know sign language too?"

"My parents and I know five different languages," Shen said. "One of them is sign language."

"Here's one more," Jean said. She opened her mouth and started making hooting and panting noises.

"What's that?" Shen asked.

"I just said 'hello' in chimpanzee!" Jean explained.

"Oh, neat!" Shen exclaimed.

Chucky started signing *snake* again.

"Come along, Chucky," Jean said. She gently took Chucky's hand. "It's time for your lesson in table manners."

" 'Bye, Chucky!" Shen said, waving as he left.

"Shen, we heard you left the breakfast early this morning," I said. "Didn't you like the food?"

Shen shrugged. "The scrambled eggs were okay," he said. "But I wanted to bring my bag of toys to the house. It was too heavy to carry around with me on the tour."

"Were you also eating a banana?" I asked.

Shen wrinkled his nose. "That's a weird question," he said. "Why do you want to know?"

The door flew open and Mrs. Tang stepped out. She was holding a shopping bag by the handle. It was full of toys—zoo toys!

"Shen," Mrs. Tang said, "please pack all your toys. We're leaving for China tomorrow."

I stared at the bag. It was completely filled with toys. Which could mean only one thing: Shen couldn't have given his toys to the orangutans!

"Okay, Mom," Shen said. He stood up and grabbed the shopping bag. Then he looked at us. "Gotta go now."

But before he went into the house, he turned and said, "And I was eating a banana . . . okay?"

Shen walked into the house and shut the door.

"Ashley, did you see how full the bag was?" I asked.

Ashley nodded. "Shen *couldn't* have thrown all his toys to the orangutans," she said, "because they were still in the bag."

"But what about the banana?" I asked. "And what if Shen lied to us about why he left the breakfast?"

Ashley wrote Shen's name in her detective notebook.

"Shen is still a suspect," she said. "But as Great-grandma Olive says, never put all your eggs in one basket."

I knew what that meant. Start looking for more clues!

"Let's check out the petting zoo next," I said, "before the zookeepers clean up any clues."

Ashley nodded. "Good idea, Mary-Kate."

To get to Hippopotamus Lane we had to

walk up Puma Path. That's where all the zookeepers' cabins are. About halfway up the path we ran into Wally again. He was standing in front of his cabin, shaking his head.

"Give me a break!" Wally wailed. "What else could go wrong today?"

"Uh-oh," I told Ashley. "Something's wrong." We ran over to Wally.

"Hi, Wally," I said. "What's up?"

Wally pointed inside the cabin. "*This* is what's up!"

Ashley and I looked inside. Then we both gasped. All the furniture in Wally's office was totally covered with green, brown, and yellow string. Sticky string!

"Another zoo toy!" I muttered.

"Just look at this mess," Wally said as we walked inside. Tim and Samantha ran in after us.

"Hi, Wally," Samantha said. "We just took down all the crossed-out posters—"

They both froze when they saw the mess.

"Yikes!" Tim cried.

"Who did this?" Samantha asked.

"Probably the same person who wrecked the zoo this morning," Ashley said.

"But I came to my office right after the tour," Wally said, "and everything here was fine."

"Did you leave your office after that?" I asked.

Wally nodded. "First I helped the Zoo Crew rip down the posters," he said. "Then I got you out of the Reptile House."

"That was about five minutes ago," I thought out loud.

"Which means," Ashley said, "the zoo-wrecker was just here!"

"Come on, Ashley!" I said, running toward the door. "Maybe we can catch him!"

FOLLOW THAT TRAIL!

Ashley and I raced out of Wally's cabin. We looked to the right. Then we looked to the left. We didn't see anyone who could be the zoo-wrecker.

"Which way?" I asked.

Ashley pointed to the ground. "Look, Mary-Kate!" she said. "A piece of sticky string!"

I crouched down to check it out. The bright green string was stuck inside a crack in the cement.

"It's sticky string, all right," I said.

We walked a few feet up Puma Path and found another piece of string. Then another. And another!

"It's a whole *trail* of sticky string!" I exclaimed.

"Let's follow it, Mary-Kate," Ashley said excitedly. "Maybe it will lead us straight to the zoo-wrecker!"

We started following the trail. Before we got very far, Felicia from the Zoo Crew ran up to us waving a clipboard.

"Mary-Kate, Ashley," Felicia called, "how would you both like to join the Chucky the Chummy Chimp Fan Club?"

"A Chucky fan club?" I repeated.

"It was my idea," Felicia said, her green eyes shining. "We'll meet once a week to talk about Chucky, collect Chucky souvenirs, and sing the Chucky song!"

"What's the Chucky song?" Ashley asked.

"It's in chimpanzee!" Felicia said. "Want to hear it?"

Felicia opened her mouth. But before she could hoot out a tune, I said, "Um—that's okay, Felicia. I'll sign."

"Me too," Ashley said quickly.

"Okay," Felicia said. She handed me a yellow pen. "Sign on the line with this marker. It's Chucky's favorite!"

As we signed our names, I thought I smelled bananas. *Must be the smelly banana in our backpack*, I figured.

"Gotta go!" Ashley said when we were done.

"Thanks a ton!" Felicia said, taking the clipboard. "And remember, Chucky the Chimp is champ!"

Ashley and I giggled as we kept on walking.

"I've heard of fan clubs for rock stars and famous people," I said, "but not for a chimpanzee!"

We followed the sticky-string trail. Ashley grabbed my arm and whispered, "Don't look now, Mary-Kate, but look who's at the popcorn cart."

"Ashley!" I said. "How can I not look and look at the same time—"

"Okay, look!" Ashley said. She nudged me in the direction of the red and yellow popcorn cart. Standing in front of it was our number one suspect—Toby Tolliver!

Toby's back was to us. I could see his purple backpack hanging off his shoulder. When he stood on his toes to pay for the popcorn, I saw a tangle of string sticking to his sneaker. Brown, green, and yellow string!

"Sticky string!" I whispered. "Toby's got sticky string stuck all over his sneaker!"

We marched straight up to Toby and tapped him on the shoulder. "Hey, Toby," I said. "Can we ask you something?"

Toby glanced over his shoulder at us. "If

you want some of my popcorn," he said, "the answer is—NO!"

"We don't want popcorn," Ashley said. She pointed down at his sneaker. "We want to know how you got that stuff on your sneaker."

"What stuff?" Toby asked.

"Kind of looks like sticky string," I said.

Toby's eyes popped wide open. He looked down at the tangle of string on his sneaker. Then he began to run!

"Let's get him!" I shouted.

6

TOBY'S WEB

Ashley and I chased Toby up Warthog Way.

"Get lost!" Toby shouted back at us.

"In your dreams!" I shouted back.

When we got halfway up the path, Toby turned into the children's playground. The playground is for little kids. It has all sorts of neat stuff to climb and crawl through.

"Where'd he go?" Ashley asked, looking around.

"There he is!" I shouted.

Toby was kneeling next to the fake prairie-dog tunnel. He looked back at us, then scurried inside.

"Hold this." I tossed the detective backpack to Ashley. "I'm going after him!"

I ran to the tunnel and crawled inside. It felt like smooth plastic under my knees, but it smelled like wet dirt. When I crawled out the other side, Toby was gone!

"Where did he go?" I asked as Ashley ran over.

We looked around again. There were kids listening through fake fox ears. And more kids piling logs on a pretend beaver dam. Suddenly I saw him.

"There!" I shouted.

Ashley and I chased Toby between a rabbit hutch and a chicken coop. Then around a fishpond.

"I don't care if you are in the Zoo Crew!" a zookeeper called out. "No running in the children's playground!"

"Sorry!" I called back to her.

Ashley and I slowed down, but Toby ran faster. He ran straight to a huge web that looked like a spiderweb. It was made out of ropes.

"I said, take a hike!" Toby shouted as he started to climb up the web.

"Not until you tell us about that sticky string on your sneaker!" I shouted back. "How did it get there?"

"None of your beeswax!" Toby yelled.

"Admit it, Toby!" Ashley called. "You trashed Wally's office. And before that you trashed the whole zoo!"

Toby climbed higher and higher. When he got to the center of the web, his backpack slid off. As it hit the ground, the stuff inside spilled out.

There was a pack of gum, a pencil with a zebra eraser, football cards, and a handheld electronic game.

But then I saw something sticking out

from under a pile of paper. I looked closer and smiled. It was a can of sticky string!

"Aha!" I declared as I picked it up.

"What did you do with the other toys, Toby?" Ashley asked. "Give them to the orangutans?"

"And what about Mei Ling's posters?" I asked. "And the snakes on the loose? And the parrots—"

"I didn't do any of that stuff!" Toby interrupted. He jumped to the ground. "I just strung up Wally's office. But he had it coming!"

"What do you mean?" I asked.

"He had no right kicking me off the Zoo Crew," Toby said. "So I decided to get even."

"Did you also lock us in with the snakes?" I demanded. "So we wouldn't see you do it?"

Toby looked like he just remembered. "Oh, yeah," he said. "I guess I did that too."

Ashley and I gritted our teeth. He'd admitted to stringing up Wally's office and locking us in with the snakes. But how did we know he didn't trash the rest of the zoo too?

"Toby, where were you this morning?" I asked. "Before the zoo opened?"

"Watching *Amazing Animals*," Toby replied. "Like I do every Saturday morning."

"*Amazing Animals*?" I asked. Ashley and I *love* that TV show. We watch it every Saturday morning at eight o'clock!

"How do we know he's telling the truth?" Ashley whispered.

"I think it's time for a pop quiz," I whispered back.

Ashley and I stood over Toby as he stuffed his junk back in his bag.

"Toby," I said, "what animal was on the show today?"

"Duh!" Toby said, rolling his eyes. "A sugar glider!"

"What was his name?" Ashley asked.

Toby had to think about that one. But then he grinned and said, "Bushy-Boy!"

"He's right," I said to Ashley.

So were the other things Toby told us about the show—how the host carried Bushy-Boy inside his pocket. And how sugar gliders got their name from eating tree sap!

Toby passed our quiz with flying colors. Which meant he had gotten to the zoo the same time Ashley and I had this morning— much too late to trash the zoo!

"Now do you believe me?" Toby asked.

"Yes," Ashley said. "But you're still guilty of the sticky-string crime."

"So what are you going to do?" Toby sneered. "Go and snitch to Wally?"

"You made the mess," I told him, "so you should tell Wally yourself."

"And what if I don't?" Toby demanded.

Ashley pulled the mini–tape recorder out

of our detective backpack. "No problem," she said. "Because I have your whole confession on tape!"

"What?" Toby shouted. He tried to grab the tape recorder, but Ashley held it out of his reach.

"Okay, okay, I'll tell Wally," Toby mumbled. Then he picked up his backpack and stomped out of the playground.

"I knew that tape recorder would come in handy," I said. "Good job, Ashley!"

"Thanks, Mary-Kate!" Ashley said with a smile.

We left the children's playground and made our way up Hippopotamus Lane.

"We have to solve this case before the Tangs go back to China tomorrow," I said. "So let's step on it."

"L-let's not!" Ashley stammered.

"Let's not *what*?" I asked.

Ashley pointed to the ground with a shaky hand. "Let's not . . . step on the . . . snake!"

I looked down—and froze. Curled on the path and hissing right at us was a big fat snake. And this time it wasn't a harmless little green garter snake!

"A-A-Ashley," I stammered, "what did we learn about poisonous snakes in Zoo Crew?"

A HANDY CLUE

"**U**m." Ashley gulped. "Poisonous snakes have slits for eyes. Nonpoisonous snakes have round eyes. Wh-what else?"

"Er," I said in a shaky voice, "poisonous snakes have diamond-shaped or triangular-shaped heads."

The snake stretched its head toward us. It had round eyes and its head didn't look like a diamond or a triangle.

"Whew!" I breathed a sigh of relief. "It's probably not poisonous."

"Then what kind of a snake is it?" Ashley asked.

I gave the snake a closer look. There was something familiar about it—as if I had seen it before. . . .

"Ashley, what does a boa constrictor look like?"

"Boa constrictor?" Ashley asked. "Their scales are either cream, tan, brown, or black with broken patterns. They don't have fangs. And they're not poisonous."

The snake curled lazily on the path. That's when I knew exactly who it was. . . .

"Hey!" I said, smiling. "That's no poisonous snake. It's Sylvia!"

Sylvia is the zoo's friendly boa constrictor. She is so friendly that Jasmine, the snake handler, lets the kids on the Zoo Crew pet her!

"What's she doing out of her tank?" Ashley asked.

Jasmine hurried up to us. She looked

totally relieved to see Sylvia. "There she is," she said. "I was looking all over the place for her!"

"How do you think she got out of her tank?" I asked.

"The person who let out the garter snakes must have let Sylvia out too," Jasmine guessed. "She just took a bit longer to crawl outside."

"We'll put Sylvia back in her tank for you," I told Jasmine.

Ashley and I lugged Sylvia to her big glass tank in the Reptile House. Jasmine held the lid open as we carefully lowered her in.

"Sylvia must be hungry," Jasmine said. "I'll go get her some rats to eat."

That sounded gross to me. But Sylvia jutted her tongue out as if to say "Bring it on!"

"Home, sweet home, Sylvia," I said.

Just as I was about to step back, I noticed something on the glass. It looked like a handprint.

"Look at that!" I said, pointing to the glass. "We must have missed it when we were looking for clues before."

Ashley tilted her head as she studied the print. "That's weird," she said. "One of the rules is no hands on the glass."

"The print couldn't be from a guest," I said. "The Reptile House was closed all morning."

"And it can't be from Jasmine," Ashley said. "She wears gloves."

I kneeled down next to the handprint. There was something weird about it, but I couldn't tell what. Until I placed my own hand up against it . . .

"Ashley!" I gasped. "Look how long the fingers are!"

Ashley stared over my shoulder at the handprint. She whistled through her teeth. "What we just found is a really big handprint!" she said.

"Yeah," I said. "And a huge clue!"

8

PAWS AND CLAWS

"**I**'ll sketch the handprint," Ashley said. She pulled her detective notebook out of my backpack. "You look around for more clues."

As I searched the Reptile House I saw the snakes coiled in their tanks. If only they could talk and tell us who had left the banana peel. And that weird handprint!

"No more clues," I announced after looking around.

"Where should we look next?"

Ashley pointed to a page in her notebook. "The petting zoo is next on the list," she said. "Let's go for it."

Ashley and I walked to the petting zoo. There were no guests inside—just Tim, Samantha, Robbie, and Melissa.

Samantha was chasing a rabbit hopping around the pen. Tim was picking up bottles that were scattered on the ground.

Ashley and I waved hello to everyone, then started looking for suspicious footprints. The only problem was there were dozens—maybe hundreds—of prints!

"Wow!" I said. "Usually when we look for footprints, there aren't so many!"

Ashley bent down and looked closer. "They look more like *hoof*prints."

"They are," Melissa said as she grabbed a goat. "The animals were running all over the place this morning."

"Hey, you guys!" Tim said. "That gives me an idea for a Zoo Crew quiz!"

"A Zoo Crew quiz? Now?" Samantha

cried. "But we still have so much more work to do!"

"That's exactly why we need a break!" Tim explained. He pointed to a pair of hoof-prints and said, "I see goat prints. What do you see?"

Ashley pointed to the ground and smiled. "Llama prints!" she announced.

"A burro!" Melissa called out.

Robbie pointed with his sneaker. "Looks like a Bengal tiger."

"Tiger?" we all shouted.

"Just kidding!" Robbie laughed.

We all got into it. Then I found some prints that had no hooves at all. In fact, they looked like human feet!

"What's *that* doing here?" I asked.

We crouched down and checked out the print.

"Those footprints have five toes," Ashley pointed out. "But they're much too wide to be human."

"Maybe it was another type of primate," I said. "Like an ape . . . or a monkey."

We had learned all about primates in Zoo Crew. All primates, except for spider monkeys, have five fingers on each hand and five toes on each foot. They can be apes, monkeys, and even people!

"But there *are* no apes or monkeys in the petting zoo," Samantha said.

"Unless," Tim said slowly, "it's Bigfoot!"

Samantha gave a little shriek, and everyone laughed. But I couldn't take my eyes off the footprint.

"Maybe it *is* an ape," I said.

Ashley made a sketch of the footprint in her detective notebook next to the handprint we found in the Reptile House.

"Let's compare the print with the poster in the Zoo Crew Hut," Ashley suggested. "The one that shows all the animal prints."

Ashley, Tim, Samantha, and I raced to the Zoo Crew Hut. The poster hung on the wall over a fish tank. Ashley held the sketch next to each set of animal prints. After comparing five or six, we found it— the perfect match!

"What kind of animal is that?" Tim asked.

I read what was written underneath the matching footprints. "It's a chimp!" I said.

Tim and Samantha high-fived. But Ashley looked deep in thought. "Chimps have long fingers," she said, "don't they?"

"I think so," Samantha said. "Why?"

Ashley told them all about the handprint we found in the Reptile House. Then she showed them the sketch.

"Looks like a chimp to me," Tim said, eyeing the sketch. "But how do we know for sure?"

We didn't have a poster showing animal handprints. But we did have something else. "Plaster casts!" I exclaimed, pointing to a case across the room.

We ran to a case with glass doors. Inside were molds of animal claws and hands. Wally had made them with clay called plaster of paris.

I carefully pulled one of the casts out of the case. The hand had a round palm and long fingers. And scratched into the plaster was the word *chimpanzee*. We compared Ashley's sketch to the cast.

"Another match!" Tim said.

"The handprint in the Reptile House *was* a chimp's!" Ashley declared. "And so were the footprints!"

"We also found a banana peel in the Reptile House," I said. "And chimps eat bananas."

"What does *that* mean?" Samantha asked.

"It means there was a chimp at the crime scenes," I explained. "And the only chimp who's allowed to walk around this zoo is Chucky!"

9

GOING APE!

"**M**ary-Kate!" Samantha giggled. "Are you saying that Chucky the Chummy Chimp messed up the zoo?"

I shook my head. "Chucky couldn't have crossed out Mei Ling's posters. Or let the snakes out of the tank," I said.

"But Chucky could have been in the petting zoo," Ashley pointed out. "And in the Reptile House. That's probably why he kept signing the word *snake*."

Tim threw his arms in the air. "So if

Chucky didn't mess up the zoo," he asked, "who did?"

"Maybe the person who's always *with* Chucky," Ashley said.

"You mean Jean Goodrich?" I asked.

Samantha scrunched her eyebrows. "Why would the Monkey Lady want to trash the zoo?" she asked.

"I don't know," Ashley admitted. "But as our great-grandma Olive always says, the guilty person might be the last one you expect."

"Jean couldn't have done it," I said. "She was at the breakfast with all the other zoo people this morning!"

"No, she wasn't," Tim said.

Ashley and I stared at Tim.

"How do you know?" I asked.

"Last week I asked Jean if she was going to the Tangs' breakfast," Tim explained. "I was hoping someone would save me some doughnuts. Or those little cinnamon buns—"

I rolled my eyes. Tim loves food more than anything. But this was important!

"Forget the doughnuts and muffins, Tim," I interrupted. "What did Jean say?"

"She said she wasn't going," Tim said. "She always feeds Chucky his breakfast at that time."

"Did you hear that, Mary-Kate?" Ashley asked.

"Yeah," I said. "If Jean didn't go to the breakfast, that means she was free to trash the zoo!"

"Are you going to investigate Jean?" Samantha asked.

"Right now?" Tim asked excitedly.

I glanced at the clock in the hut. "We'll do it tomorrow," I said. "Ashley and I have to go home and take care of our own animal."

"Our dog, Clue!" Ashley said.

"And *we'd* better go back to the petting zoo and clean up," Samantha said.

"Not before I buy a bag of peanuts," Tim said.

"To feed the elephants?" I asked.

"No!" Tim patted his stomach. "To feed *me*!"

Ashley and I said good-bye to our friends. On the way to the gate we saw Shen and Chucky signing to each other. Jean was smiling as she watched.

"Why would Jean trash the zoo?" Ashley wondered out loud.

"I don't get it either," I said, shaking my head. "Her business is monkeys, not monkey business!"

The next morning Ashley and I met Tim and Samantha outside the zoo gate. After showing our Zoo Crew passes to the guard, we went into the zoo.

The first person we saw was Toby Tolliver.

Oh, no! Was he here to make more trouble?

"Hey, Toby," I called. "What are you doing here?"

Toby scowled. "Wally's making me clean up the mess I made in his office," he said. "And it's all your fault!" He stomped away.

Ashley and I grinned at each other. We walked on.

Mr. Farley was standing outside his house. He was watching the Tangs load their luggage into the trunk of their car.

"Are the Tangs really leaving, Mr. Farley?" Tim asked.

Mr. Farley nodded. "I tried to get them to stay," he said, "but they're leaving in an hour."

An hour? That wasn't a lot of time to crack a case. So we would have to work fast!

"Let's search Jean's office," I told Ashley.

On our way to the cabins, I saw Jean. She was standing next to Chucky as he signed for a bunch of guests. Shen was watching with a big smile on his face.

"Perfect," Ashley said softly. "Jean is busy."

"Let's hope she stays that way while we search her office," I said.

"Tim and I can make sure Jean is busy," Samantha offered. "We can keep asking Chucky to say things in sign language."

"And translate it into chimpanzee," Tim said. "That ought to keep her busy!"

Tim and Samantha ran over to Jean. Ashley and I ran straight to Jean's office. It was the only cabin with monkey wind chimes over the door.

The door was halfway open. We peeked inside . . . and saw Felicia!

"Hi, guys!" Felicia said cheerily. She was standing on a chair and writing on a big wall chart. "I was just writing up Chucky's schedule!"

I looked over at Ashley. How were we going to search Jean's office with Felicia around?

"See?" Felicia asked. "Chucky has a signing demonstration at ten, picture-taking at eleven, and—"

Felicia suddenly stopped. "Uh-oh!" she said. "Chucky's insect break is at ten-thirty. And it's my job to bring the insects!"

She put down her marker and picked up a glass jar. It was filled with the creepiest-crawliest bugs!

"Chucky loves a big, juicy dung beetle!" she said. "See you!" She picked up the jar and rushed out of the cabin.

"Alone at last," Ashley said. "Let's look for clues!"

Ashley and I looked all over Jean's office. The walls were covered with posters and photos of Chucky. Jean's shelves were filled with chimp-training videos and stuffed chimpanzees. I found tons of books about chimpanzees, even one written by Jean herself!

"Nothing suspicious yet," I said. "Just a lot of chimp stuff."

"That's what you think," Ashley said. She was smoothing out a crumpled piece of paper on Jean's desk. "Look what I just found in Jean's trash can!"

I ran to Ashley and looked over her shoulder. The paper was a newspaper article. The headline read: MOVE OVER, CHUCKY, AND MAKE ROOM FOR MEI LING!

Ashley read part of article out loud: "'If Mei Ling comes to the California Zoo, Chucky the Chummy Chimp will no longer be top banana!'"

It suddenly hit me. "Ashley! Maybe Jean is jealous of Mei Ling for taking attention away from Chucky!"

"Sounds like a motive to me," Ashley agreed.

Motive is a word that Ashley and I use a lot. It means a reason for doing something.

"And remember the parrots?" I asked. "Maybe they were repeating Jean saying, 'I hate Mei Ling!'"

The monkey chimes jangled as the door swung open. Ashley and I spun around. But it wasn't Jean or Chucky or Felicia. It was Wally!

"I thought I saw you two go in here," Wally said, smiling. "How's the case coming along?"

Ashley and I ran over to Wally. We showed him the article and told him everything we found out about Jean.

"Jean had plenty of time to trash the zoo yesterday, Wally," Ashley said excitedly.

"Because she wasn't at the Tangs' breakfast!" I added.

I waited for Wally to smile or look excited. But instead, he looked totally confused!

"Jean can't be the zoo-wrecker," Wally said. "She loves the zoo and she wouldn't do anything like that. Besides, Jean *was* at the breakfast."

"She what?" Ashley and I cried at the same time.

"I saw her myself," Wally said. "She was pigging out on everything. First she ate all the bran muffins. Then she grabbed the last mushroom omelet!"

Ashley turned to me. "If Jean was at the breakfast yesterday . . . then who was with Chucky?"

Ashley and I put our heads together to think.

Then at the same time we both said, "Felicia!"

DID SHE? OR DIDN'T SHE?

"**F**elicia is the zoo-wrecker?" Wally asked, surprised.

"Jean is always giving Felicia special jobs to do for Chucky," I explained.

"Maybe Jean put Felicia in charge of Chucky while she went to the Tangs' breakfast," Ashley said.

"Felicia could have given Chucky a banana to keep him busy," I added. "While she trashed the zoo!"

"But why would she trash the zoo?"

Wally asked. He looked very serious.

"For the same reason we thought Jean did," Ashley said. "There's just one problem. We don't have any proof."

There it was again—the *P* word. But Ashley was totally right. We couldn't accuse Felicia just because she sometimes takes care of Chucky! We had to think up a plan.

The three of us left Jean's cabin. We walked up Puma Path and turned onto Hippopotamus Lane. Most of the crossed-out posters of Mei Ling were gone except for one.

"They forgot this one," I said. I grabbed the poster and started to rip it down when I smelled something familiar. . . .

"Ashley?" I said. "Is that stinky banana peel still in our backpack?"

Ashley was wearing the detective backpack today. She shook her head. "I left it in our office this morning because it was way too stinky. Why?"

I gave the poster a few quick sniffs. "This poster smells like bananas," I declared. "And Felicia's marker smelled like bananas too!"

Ashley sniffed the poster. Then she smiled and said, "Mary-Kate, Wally, I think we have our proof!"

"Now let's find Felicia!" I said.

We found Felicia with Chucky near the zoo gate. Tim and Samantha were there too. And so was Shen. He was wearing Chucky's cap.

"Get your picture taken with Chucky the Chummy Chimp!" Felicia called out. She pointed to a man holding a camera. "No autographs, please. Just pictures!"

"Felicia," I said as we walked over, "did Jean ask you to watch Chucky yesterday morning? During the breakfast?"

Felicia blinked a few times. Then she said, "Maybe . . . I do lots of things for Chucky."

"Eee, eee, eee!" Chucky cried. He started jumping up and down and signing.

"That means snake!" Shen said proudly.

"Um—I read Chucky a story yesterday morning!" Felicia blurted out. "And it was about snakes—right, Chucky?"

Chucky slapped his forehead with his hand.

"That means 'Give me a break!'" Shen said.

Mr. and Mrs. Tang and Mr. Farley walked over.

"Shen," Mr. Tang called, "we're going to the airport."

"Mr. and Mrs. Tang, please wait," Wally told them. "I think you'll want to hear this."

"Hear what?" Felicia asked in a worried voice.

"Felicia, we found Chucky's prints at all of the places that were trashed yesterday," I said.

Felicia's eyes widened. "Chucky must

have walked away from me when I wasn't looking," she said quickly.

"Does he also draw *X*'s?" I held up the poster with the *X* mark on it. "With markers that smell like bananas?"

"Rats," Felicia muttered.

"Felicia!" someone exclaimed. "You didn't!"

Ashley and I spun around. Jean was standing behind us. She looked surprised.

"Well, Felicia?" Jean asked. "Were you the person who did those terrible things?"

Felicia bit her lip. Her eyes darted this way and that. But then she looked at us and declared, "Okay, I did it! But I did it for Chucky!"

"Chucky?" Jean asked. "What do you mean?"

"I didn't want Mei Ling to be the star of the zoo," Felicia confessed. "So I did the only thing I could think of to keep her from coming here!"

I looked sideways at Ashley. We were right about Felicia and her motive!

"It's wonderful that you love Chucky so much, Felicia," Jean said. "But the zoo can learn a lot from having a panda too."

The Tangs looked confused.

"What is going on, please?" Mrs. Tang asked.

I heard Wally explain everything to the Tangs. He even mentioned Ashley's and my names.

"I'm sorry, everyone," Felicia said. "Because of me Mei Ling will never come here."

"Who says she won't?" Mr. Tang asked.

"What did you say?" Mr. Farley asked.

"Now we know that your zoo isn't always like a circus," Mr. Tang said with a smile.

"And if two children can work so hard to prove it," Mrs. Tang said, "then this is the zoo for our Mei Ling!"

"Hot dog!" Mr. Farley pumped his fist in the air and cheered, "We're getting a panda! We're getting a panda!"

Everyone started to cheer—even Shen!

"Mom, Dad?" Shen asked. He put his arm around Chucky. "Can we take Chucky back to China with us?"

"Chucky?" Mrs. Tang asked.

"I like Chucky!" Shen said. "He even gave me his cap!"

Chucky smiled at Shen with huge white teeth.

"We never had a signing chimpanzee in our zoo before," Mr. Tang said.

"Chucky has never been to China either," Jean said.

Ashley and I glanced at each other.

"I know!" Ashley said. "Why doesn't Chucky go to China when Mei Ling is sent to America?"

"Sort of like an animal exchange program!" I said.

"And I can go with Chucky," Jean said, "to study the primates of China."

"A wonderful idea!" Mrs. Tang declared.

Felicia walked over to Chucky. "I'll miss you, Chucky," she said as she signed the words.

Chucky signed back. "I'll miss you too," Jean translated.

Mr. Farley followed the Tangs back to the house. This time, he was smiling. So was Wally as he walked over to us.

"You two really *are* good detectives!" Wally said. "How did you solve this case just in the nick of time?"

Ashley and I smiled our biggest smiles.

"We just used our detective skills!" Ashley said.

"And," I added, "our *animal instincts*!"

Hi from both of us,

The week before Easter Ashley and I took part in the big Easter Egg Race in the park. The person who found the most golden Easter eggs and crossed the finish line first won the chance to star in a television commercial!

We didn't win the race—Casey Bailey did. But then everyone said she cheated! It was up to Ashley and me to prove that she didn't. What to find out what happened? Check out the next page for a sneak peek at *The New Adventures of Mary-Kate & Ashley: The Case Of The Easter Egg Race.*

See you next time!

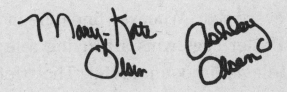

The Case Of The
EASTER EGG RACE

"I see an egg!" my twin sister, Ashley, cried. "Come on, Mary-Kate!" She skated over to a tree and scooped up a golden egg from the grass underneath it. Ashley placed it safely in her basket.

"Cool!" I gave my sister a high five. "Now we both have one."

Ashley and I were in the big Easter Egg Race in the park. The owner of Rudy's Roller Rink, Rudy Rizzo, holds the race every year. Whoever finds the most golden Easter eggs wins a starring role in Rudy's television commercial. The tricky part is that everyone in the race has to wear roller skates—and if you drop an egg, it doesn't count.

SCREECH! We heard a loud whistle. That meant the race was over! Ashley and I skated toward the finish line with our egg baskets as fast as we could.

We crossed the finish line. Adam, Casey, and Brett were already there.

"Good job, girls," Rudy said.

"Thanks, Rudy!" Ashley said.

When all the other kids crossed the finish line, Rudy started counting up the eggs. A few minutes later, he announced, "Casey Bailey is the winner! She found nine eggs— the most anyone ever found in the history of the race!"

Casey jumped up and down and screamed, "I knew I'd win! I knew it! I knew it! I knew it!"

We all clapped. Our friends Patty, Tim, and Zach skated up to us.

"Look at her," Patty said, pointing to Casey. She was posing for a picture with Rudy and the mayor. "Casey thinks she is so great."

"Yeah," Tim said. "I don't want to sound like a sore loser—but Casey is acting like a sore winner!"

"It's not fair," Zach Jones muttered. "There's no way anyone could find nine eggs! Unless . . . "

"Unless what?" I asked.

BEEP! A car horn honked. Our mom was here to pick us up. Ashley and I waved good-bye to our friends and skated to the car. All the way home, I wondered what Zach had meant—unless what?

After lunch Ashley and I headed upstairs to our attic office—the headquarters of the Olsen and Olsen Detective Agency. Our silent partner, our basset hound, Clue, was snoozing on the couch. We sat down and started making Easter baskets for our little sister, Lizzie.

Suddenly there was a knock on the door.

"Quick, hide everything! It's Lizzie!" Ashley whispered. We shoved our baskets, the decorations, and the bags of chocolate eggs under our side-by-side desks.

"Come in!" I called.

The door burst open. It wasn't Lizzie. It was Casey—and she was crying!

"Please, Mary-Kate and Ashley, I need your help!" Casey said. "Rudy says I cheated in the race and now I can't be in the commercial!" She sniffed. "But I didn't cheat! And I want you guys to prove it!"

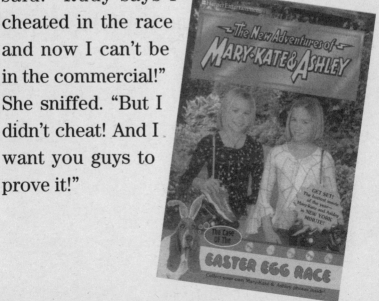

GO Shopping in Style!

$250 value

One lucky Grand Prize Winner will win a $250 gift check, plus a backpack from the *mary-kateandashley* brand!

MARY-KATE AND ASHLEY
Shopping Spree Sweepstakes

OFFICIAL RULES:

1. No purchase necessary.

2. To enter complete the official entry form or hand print your name, address, age, and phone number along with the words "MARY-KATE AND ASHLEY Shopping Spree Sweepstakes" on a 3" x 5" card and mail to: MARY-KATE AND ASHLEY Shopping Spree Sweepstakes, c/o HarperEntertainment, Attn: Children's Marketing Department, 10 East 53rd Street, New York, NY 10022. Entries must be received no later than May 31, 2004. Enter as often as you wish, but each entry must be mailed separately. One entry per envelope. Partially completed, illegible, or mechanically reproduced entries will not be accepted. Sponsors are not responsible for lost, late, mutilated, illegible, stolen, postage due, incomplete, or misdirected entries. All entries become the property of Dualstar Entertainment Group, LLC, and will not be returned.

3. Sweepstakes open to all legal residents of the United States (excluding Colorado and Rhode Island), who are between the ages of five and fifteen on May 31, 2004, excluding employees and immediate family members of HarperCollins Publishers, Inc., ("HarperCollins"), Warner Bros.Television ("Warner"), Parachute Properties and Parachute Press, Inc., and their respective subsidiaries and affiliates, officers, directors, shareholders, employees, agents, attorneys, and other representatives (individually and collectively "Parachute"), Dualstar Entertainment Group, LLC, and its subsidiaries and affiliates, officers, directors, shareholders, employees, agents, attorneys, and other representatives (individually and collectively "Dualstar"), and their respective parent companies, affiliates, subsidiaries, advertising, promotion and fulfillment agencies, and the persons with whom each of the above are domiciled. Offer void where prohibited or restricted by law.

4. Odds of winning depend on the total number of entries received. Approximately 250,000 sweepstakes announcements published. All prizes will be awarded. Winner will be randomly drawn on or about June 15, 2004, by HarperCollins, whose decisions are final. Potential winner will be notified by mail and will be required to sign and return an affidavit of eligibility and release of liability within 14 days of notification. Prize won by minors will be awarded to parent or legal guardian who must sign and return all required legal documents. By acceptance of their prize, winners consent to the use of their names, photographs, likeness, and biographical information by HarperCollins, Parachute, Dualstar, and for publicity purposes without further compensation except where prohibited.

5. One (1) grand prize winner will win one (1) gift check plus one (1) *mary-kateandashley* brand backpack. Approximate retail value of the total prize is $250.00.

6. All prizes will be awarded. Only one prize will be awarded per individual, family, or household. Prizes are non-transferable and cannot be sold or redeemed for cash. No cash substitute is available. Any federal, state, or local taxes are the responsibility of the winner. Sponsor may substitute prize of equal or greater value, if necessary, due to availability.

7. Additional terms: By participating, entrants agree a) to the official rules and decisions of the judges, which will be final in all respects; and to waive any claim to ambiguity of the official rules and b) to release, discharge, and hold harmless HarperCollins, Warner, Parachute, Dualstar, and their respective parent companies, affiliates, subsidiaries, and advertising, promotion and fulfillment agencies from and against any and all liability or damages associated with acceptance, use or misuse of any prize received in this sweepstakes.

8. Any dispute arising from this Sweepstakes will be determined according to the laws of the State of New York, without reference to its conflict of law principles, and the entrants consent to the personal jurisdiction of the State and Federal courts located in New York County and agree that such courts have exclusive jurisdiction over all such disputes.

9. To obtain the name of the winner, please send your request and a self-addressed stamped envelope (residents of Vermont may omit return postage) to MARY-KATE AND ASHLEY Shopping Spree Sweepstakes Winners, c/o HarperEntertainment, 10 East 53rd Street, New York, NY 10022 by July 1, 2004 Sweepstakes Sponsor: HarperCollins Publishers, Inc.

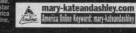